6/94

D0570726

T2-CAY-032

FIREBIRD

BUILT WITH EXCITEMENT!

BY JAY SCHLEIFER

Crestwood House
New York
Maxwell Macmillan Canada
Toronto
Maxwell Macmillan International
New York   Oxford   Singapore   Sydney

Crestwood House
Macmillan Publishing Company
866 Third Avenue
New York, NY 10022

Maxwell Macmillan Canada, Inc.
1200 Eglinton Avenue East
Suite 200
Don Mills, Ontario M3C 3N1

Macmillan Publishing Company is part of the Maxwell Communication
Group of Companies.
Produced by Twelfth House Productions
Designed by R Studio T
Photographs by Jeff Greenberg

First edition

Printed in the United States of America

10   9   8   7   6   5   4   3   2   1

Library of Congress Cataloging-in-Publication Data

Schleifer, Jay.
Firebird / by Jay Schleifer. — 1st ed.
p.   cm.—(Cool classics)
Summary: Discusses the history and dynamics of the popular
sports car made by General Motor's Pontiac division.
ISBN 0-89686-702-1
1. Firebird automobile—History—Juvenile literature.   2. Firebird
automobile—Juvenile literature.   [1. Firebird automobile—History.]   I. Title.   II. Series.
TL215.F57S35   1993
629.222'2—dc20   92-15069

CONTENTS

Since 1967, Pontiac's sleek Firebird has been a dream machine anyone can own.

1 KNIGHT RIDER

The picture on your TV set shows a vast desert. As the sun sets, the sky turns a fiery red. The music you hear has a driving beat.

Then you see a car cut across the screen. It's as black as a thundercloud and just as packed with power. It streaks across the desert at fantastic speed, leaving waves of dust to mark its path.

As the camera comes closer, you see more of the car. Its nose is low to the ground. Its wedged body cuts the air like a sword. The windows are blacked out so you can't see the driver. But that doesn't matter. The car is the star here.

You notice the red beam of light on the nose. It sweeps back and forth as though it were hunting...and it is! The car is searching for evil to fight and wrongs to right. If you haven't guessed by now, this is KITT—the amazing, talking, flying, superstar car of the TV show "Knight Rider."

Back in the 1980s, "Knight Rider" was one of the most popular shows on TV. It's still seen in reruns nationwide.

When the producers decided to make the show, they knew the car they cast as KITT had to be special. The car would be the real star of this show. But they also knew that many copies of KITT would be destroyed in stunts like crashing and flying. Even with a Hollywood-sized budget, the show's producers couldn't afford to build all these cars from scratch. Instead, they needed a dream car they could order by the dozen right from a factory. They needed an ordinary car that could play the part of a billion-dollar, one-of-a-kind special.

Luckily, there was such a car. KITT was a slightly modified Pontiac Firebird Trans Am.

TV viewers passed Birds like KITT on the street every day. Yet they never had a problem believing a Firebird could have all of KITT's fantastic powers. For the thousands of people who've driven Firebirds since they first were built in 1967, the Bird is a special car.

This is its story.

2 HOW EXCITEMENT GOT STARTED

For years, Pontiac's motto has been "We Build Excitement!" And most fans who've driven Firebirds, GTOs and other hot Pontiacs believe that the company has delivered on that motto. But to understand where cars like this came from, you need to know the background of Pontiac. That includes the surprising fact that it used to be General Motors' dullest division!

First named Oakland, the Pontiac once had all the fire and flash of a gray winter day. It was a car Chevy buyers bought when they got older and made a little more money. For buyers like these, Oldsmobiles and Buicks were too flashy, and Cadillacs were for movie stars and millionaires. No, a nice, quiet Pontiac was just fine, thank you. It had softer seats and a little more chrome than the old Chevy.

Car companies often use racing in their ads to sell cars. Pontiac's ads were unexciting. They boasted that their car "won first place in the *reliability* race"!

True racing fans called Pontiacs "the old folks' car" or "Chevies without teeth."

That began to change in the late 1950s, when Pontiac got a new boss. His name was Semon Knudsen, but most people called him "Bunky." Knudsen's father had once been president of GM, so

In the 1950s, Pontiac was known for building dull cars.

Pontiac workers welcomed Bunky Knudsen as an old friend when he came on board. Little did they know he was about to change their world!

Knudsen's mission was to sell more cars than Pontiac ever had. To do it, he had to reach new kinds of buyers.

He knew where to find them. The 1960s would be the decade of the young American. Millions of babies born after World War II were about to reach car-buying age. And whatever brand of car could catch their attention would certainly do well in the years ahead.

Knudsen knew exactly what they wanted. Young people everywhere were looking for hot-looking, performing cars. Knudsen decided that Pontiac should build such cars. But to do it, the company needed to change its style and get some excitement into its soul.

It didn't take long for Knudsen to get his message to Pontiac workers. When he arrived, the 1958 model was just about to be built. Knudsen took a look at it. It was a big Plain Jane of a box, with two chrome stripes running down the hood. These "silver streaks" were part of the Pontiac look. Every model since the 1930s had had them.

Knudsen looked at the faces around him. They were all waiting to see what he thought of their pride and joy. Then he dropped the bomb. "Take the silver streaks off," he ordered.

The workers couldn't believe what they were hearing.

First, it was already too late to make such changes. And second, Knudsen was asking them to remove Pontiac's brand on the car. But the streaks came off. And at that moment, Pontiac began to become the car it is today.

In the next few years, the performance of Pontiacs improved. There were "wide-track" sedans, with special mods to make the **suspension** wider for better handling. Hot-rodded engines, up to 455 **cubic inches** in size, were added. The model names were taken from racing, like Bonneville, Grand Prix and Le Mans. And the factory backed races such as **NASCAR** stock-car races and **NHRA** drag races. In every way, the cars got faster, cleaner and meaner.

Once somebody asked Knudsen if he were going to lose Pontiac's older buyers as he brought in younger buyers. He then shared his secret of success. He intended to *keep* many of the older buyers! Knudsen felt they were young at heart, no matter what their age. They wanted exciting cars too!

"You can sell an old man a young man's car," said Bunky Knudsen. "But you can *never* sell a young man an old man's car."

Sedans like this 1964 GTO helped change Pontiac's dull image. Ads called this car the "Tiger."

 3 **TAKE THE CAMARO AND MAKE A CAR OUT OF *THAT*!**

One of the most important changes Knudsen brought was one that buyers did not see. He hired new designers and engineers. Many of them were sports-car lovers who wished that Pontiac would build its own sports car. They wanted a two-seater to rival Chevy's Corvette.

They designed it several times, mostly for their own enjoyment. The designers drew up the car of their dreams, then modeled it in clay. The engineers developed plans to make it run.

But deep down, these people knew that GM would never allow them to build such a car. GM's top executives favored big sedans and big profits. They didn't understand sports cars and didn't want to. Auto writers were amazed that GM's Corvette ever made it into production. It was almost certain that there would never be *two* such cars from GM.

Then Ford, GM's biggest rival, came out with the Mustang! It showed GM executives that sports cars could make big profits. At first, top managers believed the sporty little Ford would fail. They even thought the success stories told about it had been made up. But finally the truth hit. GM knew it had to do something fast. Chevy was asked to come up with a new sports car, the Camaro, to meet the Mustang threat.

In those days, GM divisions were great rivals of each other, as well as of Ford. So it was natural that Pontiac workers scoffed at the Camaro. They thought it was a rush job. And since it was built with Nova sedan parts, they doubted it would make much of a sports car. But the Camaro gave Pontiac designers new hope that GM might allow even more sports cars. And they rushed to turn that hope into a Pontiac speedster *they* could be proud of.

No, the car they created was not the Firebird. Instead, it was a sleek two-seater called the Banshee. The car was named after a Navy fighter jet.

The Banshee was a real sports car. The buyer could choose a hot V-8 engine or a European-type **overhead cam** six. It looked like a mini-Corvette. Because it was smaller than the Vette, it was designed to sell for a lower price. It would have been the first *low-cost* American two-seat sports car, with the same appeal a Mazda

Miata or Honda CRX has today.

The key man behind the Banshee was a young engineer named John Z. DeLorean. You may have heard of him. After he left GM, he tried starting his own sports-car company. He also allegedly got involved in a drug deal while raising money for the company! DeLorean was arrested but was later found not guilty of all charges.

During the 1960s DeLorean was one of the smartest minds at GM. A few years after Bunky Knudsen was promoted, DeLorean took Knudsen's place as head of Pontiac. At only 40 years old, he was the youngest person ever to hold that job.

DeLorean loved the Banshee and pushed the idea of building it. He had drawings made, reports written and studies done. He even had three actual, running cars built, at huge cost. And he constantly brought up the subject with his bosses.

As hard as DeLorean tried, though, among executives the old feelings about sports cars were strong. GM felt that the Corvette and the Camaro were enough.

Again and again, DeLorean's project was turned down. As the months went by, DeLorean became more and more frustrated. He pushed his bosses harder to produce the Banshee. He even offered to build it as a four-seater if that would help.

Finally he got his answer. The Banshee, DeLorean was told, would never be built. It was dead, gone, finished, and he shouldn't mention it ever again!

When he got the word, DeLorean was at the design office with GM's top vice-president, a man named Ed Cole. What happened next seems hard to believe.

"They had a loud argument, right in front of the designers," reports a man who was there. "John called Cole a bunch of rude names! They turned around at that point and Cole said, 'Well, you

Pontiac designers felt the original Camaro was a Plain-Jane car. But the fabulous Firebird was modeled after it!

can take the Camaro and make a car out of *that*!'"

After Cole left, DeLorean and his people went over the wreckage of their dream. Instead of the Banshee, they were stuck with what they saw as a hand-me-down from Chevrolet!

They brought in a Camaro and checked it out. They did not like what they saw. "It was kind of a nothing, plump-looking little car," said Herb Kadeu, who worked in the design office. "It didn't have any visual horsepower."

Pontiac engineers weren't any happier with the Chevy than the designers were. It seemed that the Camaro had a kind of half frame called a **stub frame**. Pontiac felt this was not as solid as the full frames they were used to.

"I remember it was pretty shaky," says Steve Malone, who was the chief engineer at that time. "It was a real basket case when we got it. It took us four or five months to bring it to our standards."

Time was short to make any changes. And Pontiac wanted to get the car to the showrooms before Mustang and Camaro took all the buyers. "It was so late," recalls chief Pontiac designer Jack Humbert, "we had to use 90 percent of the Chevy sheet metal."

Chevy didn't make the job any easier. "They didn't really want us in the program, and we got very little help from them," says Kadeu. "We were a little like orphans, but we were going to show them what we could do!"

 THE MAGNIFICENT FIVE

Within weeks, the plump little car began to become a *Pontiac*. First, the designers added the famous split-grille front end and they pushed the nose forward. Then they wrapped the bumper around the grille and made it part of the design.

At the rear, six slot taillights were added for a new look. Make-believe vents were punched in behind the doors. Then the designers made a huge change in the car's look. And the change was one of the easiest to make!

The Camaro came with small wheels and skinny tires, unless you were willing to pay more for better equipment. So Pontiac installed wider, gutsier-looking wheels and tires as *standard* equipment. They used the famous red-striped "wide-oval" tires made famous on the GTO, Pontiac's muscle car of the 1960s. Suddenly the car took a wide stance on the road, like a champion broad jumper about to make a giant leap.

The designers also thought up a completely new idea that will be long remembered. While working on another car, they wanted to add a **tachometer**—a meter that counts engine speed. But there was no room on the dashboard. So the designers put the tach *outside* the car. It lived in a bulge out on the hood. This idea was added to the new Pontiac sportster.

Actually, it made a lot of sense. The driver could read the tach without taking his or her eyes from the road. What about days when the tach was covered with snow? "You don't drive fast enough in snow to need a tach," answered the designers with a smile.

The engineers now got into the act. They made up for the stub frame by strengthening the car in dozens of ways. The Camaro's **single-leaf** rear spring was replaced by a stronger unit. Extra metal was added in many places to provide better handling and a quieter ride. And Pontiac installed its own family of engines. They tried some V-8 engines. They also tried out the advanced over-head cam six meant for the two-seater. "We were out to make the car twice as good as a Camaro," said George Roberts, a Pontiac engineer.

By late 1965, Pontiac had turned the hand-me-down Camaro

15

The famous split grille was one of the 1968 Firebird's flashy features.

into the car they thought it should be. Now they stood back and looked at what they'd done. It wasn't the two-seater of their dreams. But they had to admit it wasn't bad.

"I've got to hand it to Jack Humbert," says Herb Kadeu. "He took this car and made it almost like something we would like to have. It sure looked a lot better than we ever thought it could. By the time it came out, we'd stopped feeling sorry for it and began to feel good about it!"

The designers and engineers had done their work. Now it was time for the advertising people to pitch in. Pontiac's car would be among the last new sporty cars, so just having such a car was no big news. There had to be something special about it. The advertisers came up with a great idea: Pontiac would come out with *five* new cars!

While not really five new cars, there would be five separate models. They ranged from a polite, low-cost 165 horsepower six-cylinder to a raging bull 325 horsepower V-8, powered with a GTO engine. By wrapping each engine choice with special trim, the different models were created. They were the Coupe, Sprint, 326, 326 HO (High Output) and the powerful 400.

There was a popular action movie at the time called *The Magnificent Seven.* It was about seven heroes. So Pontiac decided to call its new line of heroes "the Magnificent Five." And that's how they were advertised.

There was one other major task. They had to name the car. When the time came to do it, Pontiac boss John DeLorean had *his* choice ready. He wanted the car called Banshee. But besides the scowls from his bosses, there was another problem. Somebody had checked out the name, and it turned out a banshee was more than a jet fighter. According to Irish legend, a banshee is an evil spirit that appears just before somebody dies! The scramble was on for a new name—and fast!

For a while, it was Fireball, then Scorpion. But not many people liked Fireball, and a Scorpion is a poisonous stinging creature, which might have scared buyers. There are also photos of the car with the nonname GM-X on it.

The final choice was a name GM had used before, on a series of dream cars of the 1950s. That name was Firebird.

Some Native American tribes told ancient tales of such a

The big-engined Firebird 400 was just one of "the Magnificent Five."

creature. Their legends described a bird that brought "action, power, beauty and youth." (The same creature inspired Ford's Thunderbird.) Since Pontiac was a Native American name itself, it was a good fit. A **badge** was quickly designed to look like the bird of the legends. And Pontiac's new sporty car—or rather Pontiac's *five* new sporty cars—were ready in record time.

5 OFF AND FLYING!

As it turned out, the world had to wait longer than usual to see Pontiac's new car. In the 1960s, new models were usually introduced in the fall, and Chevy's Camaro reached showrooms in September 1966. But it wasn't until February 1967—a full five months later—that the Firebird took flight. The delay had been caused by Pontiac's late start and a GM decision to let Chevy have the spotlight to itself for a time.

When the Bird finally did take off, it really took off! The buying public could see that it was hatched from the Camaro. But Pontiacs always used a lot of Chevy parts. A sports car seemed to fit Pontiac's image well. After all, Pontiac was GM's performance brand.

Firebird ads went straight for the speed lover. "If you can stop drooling for a moment, we'd like to tell you what's propelling the Firebird in the picture," one ad read. It went on to talk about the Firebird 400, the hottest V-8 model. Then the ad ended with, "Of course, if the 400 is too much car for you, there are four other Firebirds. Lucky you."

Performance was as hot as promised. A 400 model ran from zero to 60 miles per hour in just over seven seconds, and hit 100

19

miles per hour in just over 17 seconds. And beefing up the springs paid off in solid handling.

Top racing drivers checked out the new car and liked it. Mario Andretti was a big fan of the hood-mounted tach. "I'm going to suggest putting this on the cars I race," he noted.

Many of the experts who tried the car sensed how much Pontiac had improved the Camaro. "Where Chevrolet ended, Pontiac started," wrote *Car Craft* magazine.

And where Pontiac ended, the customers began. In a month, more than 30,000 Firebirds were sold. Sales for the year totaled 82,560, even though the "year" for Pontiac had started five months late.

These numbers weren't close to those posted by the Mustang, which had over 442,000 sales, or the Camaro, which reached 201,000. But it's not really fair to compare. There are far fewer Pontiac dealers than Chevy or Ford. Instead, it is fair to say that the Firebird was off and flying!

6 SUPERBIRD...THE TRANS AM

Almost as soon as their Bird tumbled out of the nest, Pontiac engineers began to think about racing it. They wanted to see how their creation stacked up against Mustangs, Cougars, Barracudas and even Camaros.

There was a perfect way to find out. Special races had been started for Mustang-sized cars, or "**pony cars**," as many people called them. This was the Trans-American Series, usually called the Trans Am. The races were sponsored by the Sports Car Club of America. In its first few years, the Trans-Am Series had been a runaway for Mustang.

For Pontiac, there were three major problems in entering. First, Trans-Am rules allowed engines up to 302 cubic inches in size. But the smallest Pontiac V-8 was 326 inches. Second, where Ford or Chevy had millions to spend on racing, Pontiac had a much smaller budget. And finally, GM was against it. Ford Motor Company actively backed their Mustangs in races. But top executives at GM told Pontiac (and Chevy) managers that anyone caught racing or openly helping others race would lose his or her job!

So there was no engine, no money and no support from the boss. That would put a crimp in anyone's racing program!

Even with these handicaps, Pontiac still looked for a way to push the Firebird's jutting nose over a finish line. DeLorean started a new group inside Pontiac to think about superperformance ideas.

This "special projects group" included a very talented engineer named Herb Adams. For a while, Adams worked with an English race-car builder. They tried to create a racing Firebird, but it failed. Then Adams tried building a small V-8 racing engine on his own, but there was not enough money. Finally, he decided to build a special performance model around a hot-rodded version of the overhead cam six.

Adams called the car the Pontiac Formula Sprint Turismo, or PFST. Besides the special engine, it included improvements in handling, extra vents, a rear wing and a special paint job. The car was *white with blue racing stripes*.

Adams then built more versions of the PFST, some with V-8 engines. Though it didn't look like the PFST would ever race, he hoped all the work would lead somewhere.

It did! The late 1960s were a time when all the pony-car makers came up with performance versions. Ford built the Boss 302 Mustang. Chevy built the Camaro Z-28. When it was Pontiac's turn, the car they wanted had already been designed. It was Herb Adams's PFST! The new super Firebird got many of Adams's new features, right down to its vents, wing and blue-and-white paint job.

One major change was made. By this time, Pontiac engineers had given up on entering their own cars in Trans-Am races, so they no longer needed a small engine. They now decided to stuff the new Firebird with one of the biggest engines Pontiac had. It was the highest-performing version of the whopping 400-cubic-inch V-8, usually used in the GTO. This engine then was treated to a special "Ram-Air" package to increase its power, up to 335 blazing horses.

Getting the 400 inch engine into the Firebird broke a company rule. At GM, such a big engine could not be used in a car of that size. But DeLorean made a deal with his bosses. If they let him put the 400 in the Bird, he'd put a special stopper on the engine. With the stopper, people couldn't use the engine at full power. "Of course, any owner could take that off in about thirty seconds!" said a Pontiac engineer later.

The result was a superhandling Bird with more power than any Firebird ever had. Everyone who drove it raved about it.

Several names for the car were considered. The top choices were Sebring (a Florida raceway) and Formula, which came from Grand Prix racing. Sebring was being used on a Plymouth, however, and Pontiac decided to keep the name Formula for later use. So managers then turned to their third choice. It was Trans Am, after the racing series.

Not everyone liked the name. But in the end, it didn't matter. "They could have named it 'Spot,'" says Pontiac ad man Ron Monchak, "and it still would have become a legend!"

The Bird really began to fly when sleek second-generation styling was combined with Trans Am muscle!

7 THE AMERICAN MASERATI

The men who made the original Firebird were the first to admit it. The 1967 model was a rush job. With more time, they could have turned out a better car. For the next new Bird, due out in 1970, there was more time. And the Firebird crew promised to do it right. In fact, when all was said and done, the second Bird was one of the great American classics. It was a design that still looked good after more than a dozen years on the road.

The first ideas about the new car came from John DeLorean himself. "He had an expensive Maserati that he drove around," remembers designer Bill Porter. "He said 'I want this [new Firebird] to *be* a Maserati, only for $3,000 instead of $12,000. A guy could buy four of them if he wanted to!'"

Many of the designers agreed. But there was another group who'd grown up in California, home of the hot rod, that had a different idea in mind. "We weren't as concerned with the Italian look," says designer Wayne Vieira. "We just wanted the car to say *performance.*"

When you put what the two groups wanted together, their aim was clear. They wanted to build a kind of Italian-looking hot rod!

Both groups agreed that the design of the new car should begin on the *inside.* Designers knew that before they drew so much as a hubcap they had to figure where to put driver, engine and all the other things a car carries. This idea came from hard experience. Many great designs turned lumpy and bumpy once room was made for the people and parts.

"Before we ever put clay on a model, we spent months in our vehicle packaging room," said senior designer Irv Rybicki. "I believed that if you package a car right, you're going to get a good-looking piece no matter how you shape the sheet metal."

Once all the parts fit properly, shaping the sheet metal began. But it did not happen for long in the usual place, the Pontiac design studio. Instead, the car was moved to a little-known room in the basement. The designers had decided this project would be as secret as developing a new missile.

Bill Mitchell, GM's top designer, explained: "The first car, to me, had no real look," he said. "It was a committee car. There were some top executives who'd come to the design center. One chopped the front, one chopped the back, and they just cooled it down to nothing. On the second one, we did it really fast and no one got in on it. We were in the mood, and nobody bothered us."

Irv Rybicki gave this reason: "I think the bosses were involved

The second-generation Firebird was a knockout from every angle.

[with the first Bird] because our friends at Ford were doing a whale of a job with the Mustang. But once ours was there to challenge the Mustang, they all relaxed and backed off."

Whatever the reason, the new Firebird took shape *fast* in its underground home. The first clay model was done by one man in only a week!

When it saw the light of day, it was a stunner! The car's lines were long and sleek from front to rear. And it was smooth, as if the upper and lower body had melted into each other. You could hardly tell where the top ended and the bottom began. With the name tags and Bird badges off, the car did look like a Maserati or a Ferrari. It was anything but a Pontiac!

An important part of the smooth look was that the front end had no chrome bumper. There was no separate bar to protect the car from nicks and bangs. Instead, the front of the car itself was made of an unusual plastic material called Endura. Softer than chrome, Endura bounced right back when anything hit it.

Pontiac had done TV ads about the new material. And, as usual, some viewers took things too seriously. One day DeLorean got a letter from a mother. Her son had seen in the ads that you could hit the front of a car without damaging it, so he had hit the family sedan with a baseball bat. Unfortunately, their car was *not* made of Endura. The mother demanded that Pontiac fix her car!

Pontiac designers were in love with the new look. But they knew that another group would have to love it too. This was the Camaro team from the Chevy division. To keep costs down, the two cars would again share the basic shape.

However, Chevy had already done a lot of work on a car body the two brands would share. But as it turned out, it was Pontiac that would have the final say in many ways.

Bill Mitchell was in charge of both groups. He'd been away on a long trip and hadn't seen either car for a while. As soon as he returned, he took a look at the Firebird version and loved it. Designer Jack Humbert tells what happened next.

"Mitchell just jumped up and down! He brought the Chevy designers in and showed them our car, because we'd done in a week what they'd worked on for six months. After that, we led the whole project for a long time."

At times, it must have seemed to Chevy that they'd never regain that lead. One day Camaro designers came to work and found the clay model of their version missing! Mitchell had ordered it moved to the Pontiac studio. He wanted Pontiac to solve a design problem Chevy couldn't get right.

Who won this little battle of the design studios? Everybody did. In the end, Chevy had as many good ideas as Pontiac. And though the two sister cars share size and shape, each has its own flavor. The Camaro is youthful, fun-filled and classy. The Bird, as its designers wanted, is a mix of Italian supercar and California hot rod…an *American Maserati.*

8 SHAKER HOODS AND SCREAMING CHICKENS

Once the basic design of the 1970 Firebird had been set, it was time to do the new Trans Am version. For this car, there was no question about which way to go. The TA in Trans Am had come to stand for things like "terrific acceleration" and "totally awesome"! The goal was Performance with a capital P!

The designers knew how to get it. Starting with the white paint and blue racing stripes of the first Trans Am, they added **wheel flares** and vents. Then they tacked on a rear tail that looked as if it had been lifted off a race car. This part, called a *spoiler,* forced the airflow to press against the trunk, said Pontiac. And this made the car more stable at high speeds. It looked pretty wild too!

Another item that may have made the car run better, but also looked great, was the famous "shaker hood scoop." This was a vent that was hooked directly to the top of the engine and fed air to it. The air came from the area above the hood. How did the scoop

Pontiac designers always went the extra mile when designing the Trans Am. The famous "shaker hood scoop" was connected right to the engine!

get over the hood to get at the air, you ask? Simple. It went directly *through a huge hole in the hood!* Think about that. An engine part stuck right out of the car!

Not only did this help the engine breathe, it helped the driver get a thrill. As soon as he or she started the car, the scoop began to shake with power. The more the driver revved, the more the scoop shook. Drivers loved to see this high-performance dance just outside the windshield. It was more fun to watch than the famous outdoor tach!

What the hood scoop promised, the engine below it delivered. Soon after the new car came out, Pontiac engineers again enlarged their top Trans Am engine. This time, it went to a hood-shaking 455 cubic inches!

This did *not* mean more power than before, though. America had begun to be concerned about auto-caused **air pollution.** And laws had been passed to make engines cleaner. One way to do this was to cut back on the power any given engine size could make. The new 455 put out no more horsepower than the 400 it replaced.

In fact, this was the beginning of changes in the market that affected pony cars from every stable: GM, Ford, Chrysler, even the Javelin from little American Motors. The youth boom that led to such cars was ending. The government was calling for cars that ran safer. Insurance companies were raising performance-car rates, figuring that owners with such cars had to be taking chances. And just when the new Trans Am was about to be introduced, GM was hit with a long factory strike, forcing the car to come out late as a 1970$1/2$ model. It seemed that storm clouds were gathering around cars like the Firebird.

Then in 1973, the storm hit full force. In the Middle East, several Arab countries got in a war with Israel. America backed Israel, and the Arab states hit back by shutting off the flow of oil to the United States.

Without oil, gasoline couldn't be made. Suddenly there were long lines at gas stations across America. People fought over who'd get the few gallons that could be had.

Luckily the gas shortage ended in just a few months. But no one knew when something like it might happen again. Many people felt that the monster-engined pony cars, which got 12 miles to a gallon on a good day, were the last thing America needed.

In a flash, Ford converted their Mustang into a tiny four-cylinder economy car, the Mustang II. Chrysler's Barracuda and the similar Dodge Challenger disappeared, as did AMC's Javelin.

GM thought about dropping the Camaro and Firebird. In the end it decided to keep the cars if they could be updated cheaply. But the company also figured that such cars were on their final lap. No more money would be spent to do them over again.

Now began the long, cold winter in the Firebird's story. In normal times, the 1970 model might have gone on until perhaps 1975. Then a new Firebird would have been introduced. But now GM didn't want to spend money on a new design. It was too risky. Instead, the old Firebird continued with just a few minor changes each year.

Year after year rolled forward, with the Bird caught in a time warp. Look at the 1975 or 1978 or 1981 version. Except for government-forced changes, like new safety bumpers and a change in rear-window shape, there isn't much difference. But that doesn't mean there is *no* difference. Two things were about to bring the Bird out of its comalike sleep.

The first was the arrival of a new Firebird chief designer, John Schinella. John, one of the most talented young designers at GM, loved hot-looking cars. For him, getting the Bird was a plum job.

Firebird designs didn't change much in the 1970s. But side curves were added to the rear window for a new, exciting look.

Second was that the *customer* didn't give up on the Firebird. Although sales dived during the gas shortage, they came right back. There would never be 400,000-sale years, such as the Mustang once enjoyed. But sales hung in there, just like the car. They even increased from year to year. Some sales figures went beyond the 100,000-car-a-year mark!

But for a long time this level of sales was still not enough to pay for major changes. What's more, the company's designers and engineers were busy redoing the sedan lines to make them smaller, safer and easier on gas. There was little time to spend on the pony cars.

So Schinella and his crew created new looks that were fast and cheap. They shuffled colors. They dreamed up two-tone paint ideas. And they made colored tape into wild stripe jobs.

One year, they came up with the idea of replacing parts of the roof with removable panels. The panels popped out, leaving only a center bar from windshield to rear window for strength. This was the famous **T-top**, an "almost convertible." (The original Firebird ragtop had been dropped years before.)

Through this sheet-metal shell game, there was always some new look to catch the buyer's eye and make him or her forget that the engines were getting weaker. (By 1977, the top speed of a Trans Am was just 117 miles per hour. Once it had been closer to 150 miles per hour!)

During those years, John Schinella had the idea for which he's best known. Pontiac called it part number UPC WW7 on the order blank. The rest of the auto world called it "the Screaming Chicken."

The "Chicken" was the world's biggest, baddest Firebird badge. It was made of tape and ran several feet across. If you chose it, it was plastered over the hood of your car like a horse blanket, too big to miss, too wild to ignore. When they saw it, thousands of traffic police looking down from airplanes and helicopters must have given thanks! Nothing made spotting a fast-traveling Trans Am easier!

The most famous Chicken of them all was the one in the *Smokey and the Bandit* movies.

In 1978 actor Burt Reynolds created a series of films about a modern hero of the highways. He cruised the turnpikes of the West, friend to all truckers and enemy of all crooks. His CB "handle" was

"Bandit." His mount was a wild black-and-gold T-top Trans Am.

The Bandit's Trans Am seemed to have superpowers. It could outrun anyone. It could turn sharp corners. And when it had to, the car was able to jump rivers. Of course, these stunts were strictly Hollywood magic. By the end of the film, a fleet of perfectly good Trans Ams had bitten the dust.

The Bandit movies turned out to be hits. They also turned the Trans Am into a dream car for thousands of young moviegoers. Sales zoomed. And about half of the Firebirds sold each year were Trans Ams, even though they had higher prices than the standard car. By 1979 there was even a hot turbo model. It was an incredible comeback!

9 THE THIRD BIRD

You step out of your house and head for your parking spot. Sitting there, ready to take you to work or school, is a sleek, wedge-shaped vehicle. Its nose is low to the pavement. Its headlights are hidden for a smoother front-end look. Its lines seem shaped by the wind. Its top is more glass than metal. And the rear is topped off by a spoiler wing, just like a racing car.

Is this a dream car? No. It's the third version of the Firebird.

When they set out to build the new third Bird, designers decided to leave behind the Italian styling of the second car. They'd shelve the wheel flares, scoops and tape stripes their design had collected over the years. Even the Screaming Chicken would be sent off for retirement. "The challenge when we took on this one," says John Schinella, "was to design the smoothest piece of machinery we'd ever done. A very clean, pure, high-tech look."

Did they succeed? Just park second and third version Firebirds next to each other. They look as if they come from different worlds. And they do.

In the case of the first and second Firebirds, there was no question that the cars would be front engine, rear drive. Almost all cars were built that way during that time. Front-wheel drive was almost unknown in the United States.

Nor was there a question that the car would have a V-8 engine. Back then, with gas at 30 cents a gallon, nobody worried much about gas mileage. Sports-car lovers were only concerned with high performance and that meant a bigger engine. It was the same for car size too. Bigger always seemed better in those days.

At that time, Ford and Chrysler provided the big competition.

The only foreign car around much was the plain little VW Beetle. And as for the Japanese, everyone knew they built cars. But most Americans felt they were poorly made copies of U.S. designs. Toyota sounded like a kind of toy, right?

But a lot had changed in ten years. When work began on the *new* Bird, even the most basic questions had to be asked. Should the car be front-wheel drive or rear? Should it have a four, six or an eight? What size should the car be? How could Pontiac meet the

Firebirds have sporty interiors. Note the aircraft-type dashboard lighting and turbo indicator lights on the hood scoop.

new safety and pollution laws yet still build a car that sparked fire in a buyer's soul? And last but not least, how would Pontiac handle the challenge of hot, high-tech Japanese newcomers? Such cars as the Nissan Z-car, Toyota Celica or Mazda RX-7 could run rings around the old American pony cars. Though they had smaller engines, they performed better, thanks to advanced engine design.

Work on the new Firebird was shaky. Designers started on the car in 1975, then again in 1978. More than once, the work was stopped by the need to work on the sedan lines that paid most of GM's bills.

But the work did *not* start at Pontiac. It began in the Advanced Studio, home of a special group of car builders. They didn't work for either Chevy or Pontiac. Instead, their job was to build the basic body that would later become *both* the Camaro and the Firebird. The idea was to make the work go smoother by avoiding the old Chevy–Pontiac rivalry and secrecy.

The idea worked. But the Advanced Studio still had a tremendous task. They had to replace one of the finest-looking machines ever to turn a wheel.

The first decision was on the car's size. Almost everyone agreed that this had to be a smaller, lighter Firebird. Gas had gotten expensive. A lighter car would be just as quick. It would get better mileage too. All GM cars were on a diet. The big sedans had lost a foot in length and 1,000 pounds in weight!

The next question was whether the new, smaller sportster would have front or rear drive. Either could be done. By 1980 GM would be using both layouts in its car lines.

The designers knew that front-wheel drive would allow more space inside the new, smaller body. It would also be safer in snow. And some designers, especially at Chevrolet, favored it. But others found it tough to get the kind of long, low lines they wanted with all the machinery packed at one end. Front-drive cars tended to be short and stubby.

Some engineers also felt that rear-drive cars handle better in sporty driving. Many of the world's top sports cars are rear-wheel drive.

Then there was the question of what engines to offer. Should there be a four, six or eight? Or maybe a choice of all three?

Pontiac asked its customers the questions in a survey. The answer: Make the new Bird what it had been in the past: a front-engine, rear-drive V-8 screamer packed with American-style excitement. Four- and six-cylinder engines could also be offered for those wanting a lower price and better gas mileage.

Up to this time, the Advanced Studio had worked on and off on the project. They'd been "blue skying"—coming up with wild creations (including cars equipped with sliding doors) that they knew would probably never be built. But now, in 1978, with the big questions answered, they could sensibly draw. And draw. And draw.

They tried hundreds, even thousands, of ideas. But nothing seemed quite right. Then one day, someone remembered a sketch done by young Roger Hughet, an assistant designer working in an office in the basement. (Firebirds always seemed to grow better in the basement!)

About a year before, Hughet was doodling the day away. Suddenly something in him made his hand sketch a wedge-shaped rear-drive car. It had a long, wavy fender line and a roof made mostly of glass. He looked at it, fiddled with it for several days and then took it to his boss, Bill Porter. Porter liked it, but back then, the design crew was still thinking front drive.

Now Porter decided the time was right to carry the idea to his boss, Irv Rybicki, head of GM design. "We took one look at Roger's drawing," recalls Rybicki, "and that was all I needed. I said do it full size, and it was a success from the beginning."

Within a short time, the whole building was excited. The designers had found the look they'd been searching for.

What did it was the *roof*. No production car had ever had a roof like this one, so totally streamlined, with so much glass. The rear window is one of the largest pieces of glass ever put on a car, and it is curved in three directions at once.

But Hughet's creation wasn't easy to build. Glass-company engineers had a fit when they saw what the GM designers wanted them to make. Nobody had ever shaped a piece of glass like that, much less produced hundreds of thousands of them. But the promise of selling GM all those new rear windows was enough to keep them trying.

"We went through probably 35 samples before we nailed it down," says Irv Rybicki. "But it's there and it's beautiful!" It's also strong enough to act as the car's trunk. You can slam it down without breaking it.

Once the basic body was final, it was turned over to Pontiac and Chevy designers. They'd now add the final body shaping and grille and taillight design that would dress the body as either a Firebird or a Camaro.

In some areas, they agreed on what to do. Both groups decided to make their cars **bottom feeders**. That meant the grille areas on the front would be more for decoration than for taking in air. Instead of being rammed in by the wind, most engine air would enter from quieter areas below the car. But the two groups differed on other decisions. The Camaro designers did their final shaping with crisp, sharp angles. John Schinella's crew at Pontiac chose wavy lines that flowed like hot syrup.

Details like these body-colored rims have always
given the Firebird first-class looks.

In some ways, both groups had to take less than they wanted and make deals with their bosses at GM to get the rest. Both Camaro and Firebird creators, for example, wanted four-headlight units that would pop in and out of the bodywork. But top executives felt this was too expensive. They told the designers to pick either two hidden lights or four that could be seen. Pontiac took the hidden two, Chevy the nonmovable four.

What finally rolled out of the studios was the same basic car with two very different looks. But both are superstar designs! "An absolute knockout!" said *Car and Driver* magazine of the new Firebird's look. The Camaro received similar praise.

One thing the designers hid well is how much smaller the third Bird is than the second car. The body was a full ten inches shorter and two inches narrower. Weight was reduced by some 500 pounds! With less weight to lug, the car was both faster and got better gas mileage. Yet the car looked even lower, longer and more streamlined than the bigger car it replaced.

Performance was helped by the car's wind-cheating shape. Hughet designed it to be gorgeous to the eye, but it turned out to be gorgeous to the air as well. When the final design was tested in a wind tunnel, the numbers made the engineers' eyes pop out. It was the lowest number they'd ever seen for an American production car. The new body cut through the air like a fighter jet.

With the outside created, attention turned to the **interior**. There were special designers for this, and they also knew what they wanted. Since the car looked like a jet outside, why not continue that idea within?

First, the designers looked at cockpits. They peeked inside the Concorde supersonic airliner, the space shuttle and sleek executive business jets like the Learjet or Falcon. Then they drew up their own version of a cockpit for the Firebird.

With its jetlike shape and hidden headlights, the
third-generation Firebird was aerodynamic.

The result was the most streamlined windshield ever seen on a
factory-built car. It had a sleek sunshade over the instruments. And
meters were made big and bold for easy reading. Improved seats
made this the most comfortable Firebird ever, as well.

The engineers also had their chance to improve the car. They
got rid of the old stub frame from the original, hand-me-down

Camaro body of 1967. The new car had a solid **unibody**, with modern **strut** suspension. The Trans Am version, always a good handler, would now be even better. And the standard Firebird would benefit as well.

Schinella decided to give the Trans Am a clean look. All the car's old tape labels were junked. And special "aero" body panels were added to smooth the airflow even more. The car also got flat-dish wheel covers like those on a World Speed Record car. This made the airflow even better.

For a while, Pontiac thought about changing the name to T/A. But at the last minute, they kept Trans Am.

One thing that did change was the hood. The Screaming Chicken was taken off the order blank. Pontiac felt it just didn't fit with the new look. But as soon as word got out, parts companies quickly jumped in and began to sell their own versions of the Screaming Chicken. Within three years, you could buy it at Pontiac again!

The new Firebird finally flew into showrooms as a 1982 model. And it was a smash, quickly becoming one of Pontiac's best-selling cars. It was created to last more than ten years with only minor changes. Then, if sales remained good, the plan was that a fourth Firebird would take its place.

 **A FUTURE FIREBIRD**

When the third Bird came out, its biggest plus was styling. Its biggest minus was performance. At the time Pontiac still had to work with the engines designed for pollution control. The top V-8 made only 145 horsepower! And some ordinary Toyota sedans were quicker than a Trans Am from zero to 60! But that would change as American carmakers learned how to combine clean air *and* performance as the Japanese seemed able to do.

In the last ten years there have been vast improvements. Even a standard Bird has horsepower approaching that of the 1982 Trans Am, although it uses a V-6 engine versus that car's V-8. As for V-8s, a special Trans Am called the GTA now has the same engine as Chevy's Corvette. It's a 350-cubic-inch mill pumping some 240 horsepower.

The car can go from zero to 60 in about six seconds. And it can go a quarter of a mile in just under 15 seconds. The top speed is more than 130 miles per hour. And all this happens with highway gas mileage of around 20 miles per gallon. American carmakers have learned their lessons well!

As this book is being written, the fourth Firebird is scheduled, along with the fourth Camaro, to go on sale sometime in the mid-1990s. There have been many rumors and some "spy" pictures, which may or may not be the final design. They show a car quite like the third Bird, but still smaller and lighter. The rumors say it's still rear drive and will be powered by V-6 and V-8 engines like those in the current Firebird.

The rumors also say that at least some major body parts will be made of a special plasticlike material. It is already used on GM's Saturn small car and the company's minivans. This stuff is light, strong, resists dents and will never, ever rust!

Beyond the fourth Bird, who knows? You may be able to choose electric versions, **two-cycle engines** and map-following systems that get directions from satellites in space. There will probably be enough buttons and computers for a sci-fi movie.

The drive for better performance, mileage, pollution control and safety in today's cars is strong. Customers want it. Some of it is

With the brand-new car due any moment, Firebird is firmly pointed towards the future!

required by law. Some of it is being forced by the challenge of foreign makers. And the U.S. companies want to be the best that they can be. These are all trends that will get stronger in the future.

Under all the high tech, though, there will always be the one feature Pontiac has been building since the day that Bunky Knudsen dumped the old silver streaks. It's called *excitement!* As long as it's there, the Cool Classic called Firebird will be flying high for a long, long time.

strut 42 Suspension part holding the wheel to the body.

stub frame 14, 15, 41 System of mounting wheels and engine in a car through a half frame connected to the body.

suspension 42 Parts that attach wheels to a car. They are usually made to move so they absorb road bumps.

tachometer 15, 20 A meter that counts engine speed.

T-top 32 A body style in which all the roof is made of removable panels except for a single bar linking the windshield and rear-window area.

two-cycle engine 43 Engine design that produces *two* pulses of power with each turn of the engine. Four-cycle engines produce *one* pulse per engine turn, so a two-cycle produces more power for the same engine size.

unibody 42 Method of building a car in which the body is strong enough to take the role of a separate frame and hold all the parts together.

wheel flares 27, 34 Parts added to a car's body to cover wider-than-normal tires.